This book belongs to:
_____
_____
_____

For Matt and my very patient sister, Alison.
And for my heroes, Emily, Jamie, Pat,
Emma, Lauren, Gemma and Vicki.

CATERPILLAR BOOKS
1 The Coda Centre,
189 Munster Road, London SW6 6AW
First published in Great Britain 2014
Text and illustrations copyright © Maxine Lee 2014
All rights reserved
ISBN: 978-1-84857-404-5
Printed in China
CPB/1800/0352/0114
2 4 6 8 10 9 7 5 3 1

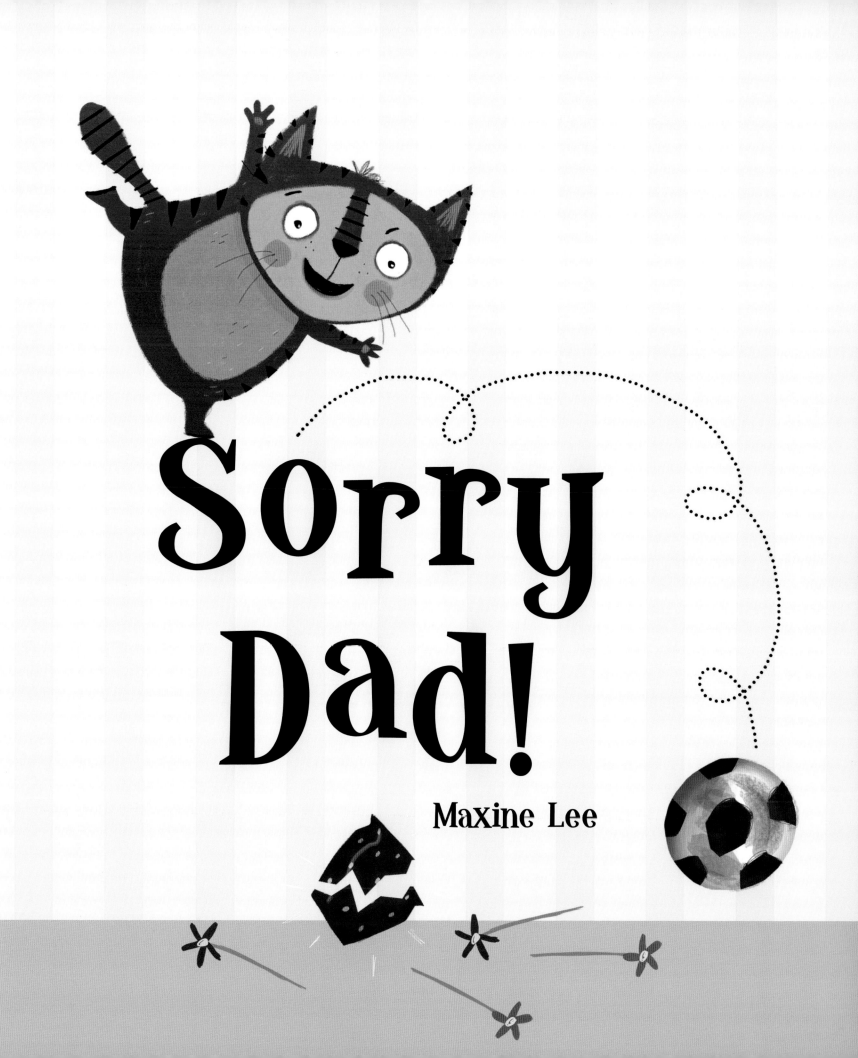

Sorry Dad!

Maxine Lee

Hello! This is me.

And this is my dad.

We are **bestest** friends.

But today he is not a happy dad...

Uh-oh!

...today he almost popped!

It all started at breakfast time,
with the battle of the Krispos.

But Dad didn't want to play.

And then I kind of sort of upset
him at lunchtime...

Shazam!

...and at
story time...

Yee-ha!

...and at tidy-up time.

After lunch, everything was fine in the garden...

until the

space

rocket

launch.

If it had gone straight up, it would have been the best launch ever!

Later, at the park, I bravely saved Dad from an attack by a bee and its stingy bottom!

Nooooo!

But he didn't
say thank you.

He said, "Home! **Now!**"

So I thought I would cheer Dad up with...

...a super, spectacular show!

Ta-da!

It was all going really
well until...

Oof!

So now I'm
sitting here.

And he's
sitting there.

I've been thinking about
ways to make it up
to him for ages and ages...

FLOWERS?

CHOCCIES?

CAR
WASH?

DINNER?

And now I've had a BRILLIANT idea!

I **think** he liked it...

After all, we are the bestest friends.